# Heaven's River

## Flairs and Glairs
Publication House

*"Heaven's River"*

## ISBN No: 978-93-90799-58-9
## 1st Edition
Language – English and Hindi

## Flairs and Glairs
**Publication House**
Regd. Under MSME Act.



Price: 299/-

# Disclaimer

This is a work of fiction and solely represent the thoughts of the corresponding authors of the articles. Our editors have tried their best to edit the content of all the authors and check the plagiarism.

All the write-ups in this book are unique and are only published in this book.

In case any plagiarism or error is found, only the author is responsible alone, and not the publisher or the Compilers.

***Cover Designing and Book Formatting***
*Shubham Shah and Ishani Agarwal*

# Acknowledgement

The completion of this anthology would'nt have been possible without the hardwork of all the core members and co-authors.

All the members behind this book have put all their hard work devoted their name and efforts for the success of this Anthology.

We are thankful to **FLAIRS & GLAIRS PUBLICATIOIN** For their constant support.
Above all a big thanks to Almighty and my parents for their support love and blessings.

# Co-Authors

**Shubham Shah (Founder Flairs and Glairs)**
**Ishani Agrawal (Co-Founder Flairs and Glairs)**

1. Raghav Chauhan (Compiler)
2. Geetika Meena
3. Kriza Monpara
4. Shubhi Gupta
5. Yukta Nawani
6. Kruti Suchak
7. Sneha Dhama
8. Anjali Maurya
9. Devika Saxena
10. Muskan Sachdeva
11. Pragya Verma
12. Samiksha Gautam
13. Archishman Satpathy
14. Agam Sachdeva
15. Narendra Kumar Rayakwar
16. Sadhwika Suma
17. Priyanka Varma
18. Ganesh Sadashiv Patil
19. Sahina Ghugha
20. Ishrat Saboon
21. Raheja Sumit
22. Kareena Verma
23. Shweta Agnihotri
24. Princy Carol Gonsalves

25. Aliya Siddiqua
26. Aishwarya Umashankar
27. Mohanapriya. K
28. M. Haseebunissa
29. Prasad Babu Galla
30. Shreya Pokhriyal
31. Deendayal Raikwar
32. Meera Vyas
33. Shaheen Ansari
34. Pratham Mittal
35. Himanshi Kamboj
36. Jasmine Panda
37. Simon Chiatante
38. Ms Daksha R Udhani

# Shubham Shah

## (Founder- Flairs and Glairs)

Shubham Shah, an entrepreneur at "Flairs & Glairs" a brand with dynamics in events organizing and cultural educational pan INDIA, is a 26yrs old guy who recently has entered the digital platform of imprinting emotions. He has initiated with his own open mic platform to help budding poets and aspiring writers under his brand named as "Teekhe Zasbaaat"

He is a commerce graduate from the Bhagalpur City of Bihar.

He states Writing has impersonated him since childhood and he has now been writing for over a decade!

Cooking, on the other hand, is his passion! He also mentions, trying out new things just tickles him!

When asked sir, Why SPICY EMOTIONS?

He smiled and added, "agar jasbaat teekhe na ho toh wo jasbaat kahan" Spices are all that blends! So do his words!

As a chef, he presents to you his dish! Hot and freshly served! Taste it! Feel it! Enjoy it! You can also find his writing in the Book "Teekhe Zasbaaat" and 50+ Co-authored anthologies. With his passion to explore opportunities across Platforms, he is working with keen devotion and We wish him all the very best for his future ventures.

He is Featured in the **International Magazine De-Mode** for his upcoming solo novel.

He is **Approved by Ne8x for its Lit Fest,** and is a **Golden Star Awards 2020 Winner.**

He is an **India Book of Records Holder** for his Anthology **Satrang,** and has the **Grandmaster** title by **Asia Book of Records**, for the same.

He has also been featured in **Prabhat Khabar, Dainik Jagran** and other renowned Newspaper for his achievements.

He has also been awarded with **India Star Republic Award 2021.**

He has been a proud co-author to

**India Book of Records (Title- Black)**

**World Book of Records (Title -15 Wonders of Poetries)**

**India Book of Records (Title - Aaina)**

**Vajra World Records Holder (Title - Gustakhi Maaf Hai)**

**High Range of Records Holder (Title - Gustakhi Maaf Hai)**

Share your reviews on his

INSTAGRAM
@spicy_emotions
@shubham4shah
Or via email on
shubham2shah@gmail.com

To stay tuned to his work and opportunities follow his business Handles

INSTAGRAM          FACEBOOK          YOUTUBE

@flairsandglairs
@teekhezasbaaat

WEBSITE:

https://flairsandglairs.in/
https://flairsandglairs.com/

# Ishani Agarwal

## (Co-Founder- Flairs and Glairs)

Ishani Agarwal hails from the City of Joy, Kolkata.
She is the co-founder of her Community "Teekhe Zasbaaat"
and Flairs and Glairs Publication.
Been a Compiler for 45+ Anthologies, she is in the process
for more. Co-authored in 150+ Anthologies. She is a India
Book of Records Holder, a Vajra World Records Holder, a
High Range of Records Holder and a Bravo Record holder.

Approved by Ne8x for its Lit Fest 2020, and Literary Icon 2020. Also a Golden Star Awards Winner 2020.

She has also been awarded with India Star Republic Award 2021.

She has been featured by the National Magazine "Taree Zameen Par" with the title 'unstoppable'.

Also featured in the International Magazine DeMode for her upcoming solo novel, she is proud to write on social issues, and is happy with the love she is receiving.

Connect with her on Instagram: @Ishani_agarwal_quotes / @compilations_so_far

# RAGHAV CHAUHAN
# (COMPILER)

Hi,

Let me introduce to **Writer Raghav Chauhan**. He is a young writer of Modern era. He was born on 06th July 1997 at Distt. Moradabad,UP. His Original name is **Mr. Ramakant Singh**.

He is 23 years old. He has started his journey of writing from **Haridwar-A holy land of Uttarakhand**. His early education was also completed from the state of Uttarakhand.

He give more importance to **ORDINARY LIFE – HIGHER THOUGHT**in his life. He struggled a lot of his life by which many newInspirations come to in his life.

He writes mostly spiritual quotes and articlesOn many topics such as **SPRITUAL KNOWLEDGE WOMEN EMPOWERMENT,NATURE, CULTURE AND CIVILIZATION, HUMAN LIFE, SOCIAL EVILS** etc.

He has also acted as co-author in 30 Anthologies under some publication like **BOOKSQUIRREL PUBLICATION,**

**FLAIRS AND GLAIRS PUBLICATION, WISDOM PUBLICATION** etc.

He has currently featured in **The On-zine Magazine** for his article **Mental Stress (A serious problem of Modern era).** Also titled as Co-compiler in 1 Anthology under Booksquirrel Publication.

He has written his solo book **Jeevan-Manthan** which is going to be publish under FnG Publication. This book is an inspirational for Human beings.

The articles or quotes written by him mainly refer to the real events of his Life which is really interesting and inspiring.

He writes mostly in Hindi (Devnagari) and his writing style is a feature of his his writing.

You can contact him on –

**Instagram - @unprofessional_writer_raghav**

**Twitter - @Raghav Chauhan**

**Facebook – Truth of life @raghavchauhan2020**

**YQ App - @Raghav Chauhan**

**Nothing is impossible in this world, you have to fight each challenge ,**

**If you got something then you have to struggle definitely.**

**Raghav Chauhan**

# GEETIKA MEENA

I am persuing my graduation from Banasthali vidyapith, I have worked as content writer in freelancer.I write poems,quotes and contents for the stories.

# **GOODNESS**

Oh dear!!
Searching for the goodness?
It's in your truthfulness!!

Why to search for the good things,
This only your loyal smile can bring!!

Do you have goodness?
Of course dear,
Just check your mindset!!

You are perfectly imperfect,
You are the stardust,
Result of billions of years!!

Where is the goodness lie,
It's the energy in you,
That can never die!!

Be away from worldly crew,
You will find goodness in you!!

# GOODNESS

What does goodness means??
Does goodness relates with greatness?

I think , answer is no!!
Why?
Because Greatness lies in goodness.
Goodness is faith in god.
Goodness is something inner peace.Greatness is outside happiness.
All educated are great persons but we can't say they are good.
To be a good person,you must have faith in god.
If you have faith in god,you will be truthful,when you are truthful,you follow right path and when you follow right paths,you automatically brighten someone's life even by troubling yourself.
That's goodness. That's real humanity!!

# GOODNESS

Once there lived a boy. His parents were only concerned about his education.

They were only concerned to make him great,but they never focused to make him good person.

Years passed and the little boy has turned out to be a strong Villain.

When he was arrested and asked why he has done it , his reply was that he had been taught to be strong,but He was not taught the path to become strong.

When he was asked why he don't use his powers in making society strong.

His reply was shocking.

He replied he had been taught to be the strongest, greatest but never taught to be kind and humble.

So, greatness is not important,how good the child is more important.

Goodness is the only way towards the good greatfulness!!

# (1)

जितना अच्छा बनना चाह,
समाज ने उतना ही बुरा करार किया।

क्या खुद के सपने जीना चाह,
इसलिए मुझे बुरा करार किया?

क्या लडकी समाज-ए-मर्यादा में ना रही,
इसलिए उसमें कोई अच्छाई नहीं रही।

क्यूँ किसी को अच्छाई के तराजू में तौलना?
क्यूँ समाज मर्जी का काम अच्छाई में नहीं मानता।

अच्छाई करना है तो किसी के रास्ते की बाधा ना बनो।
अच्छाई करना है तो डूबते का किनारा बनो।

# KRIZA MONPARA

She is Kriza b Monpara she is 10 years old writer she is form surat she is a by professional freelance writing all type content language in Hindi Gujarati and English.

## (1)

तू है मेरे प्यार का अनोखा राज इसीलिए तुझ पर है मुझे विश्वास
हो सके तो बन जाना मेरे खास बन कर आऊंगी मैं तेरी तेरे पास
उम्मीद रखो प्यार की प्यार की होगी जीतकभी कभी कभी कभी
अपनों को बेगाना कर जाती है ऐसी है दुनिया की रीत
रह सके तो रह लेना मेरे बगैर वरना मैं किसी को छोड़कर आऊंगी
तेरे पास
इतना तू है मेरे लिए खास किसी और पर ना होगा मुझे विश्वास
तेरे लिए सब सजाऊंगी तारे अंबर से तोड़ लाऊंगी

## (2)

जिंदगी की वह उम्मीद है तू
ना छूट सके ऐसी आदत है तू
ना तुझे पा सके ऐसी हसरत है तू
जो पा कर भी को दे ऐसी चाहत है तू
जिंदगी की वह उम्मीद है तू
ना छूट सके ऐसी आदत है तू
तुमको तो मिल जाएगा साथी अपना हम किसी को नहीं बन सकेंगे
हम सफर अपना
अपनो की महफिल में बेगाने हुए हम
तेरी चाहत के दीवाने हुए हम
तुझे पा ना सके तो क्या हुआ
तेरी हर एक अंछुवन ने मुझे छुआ

(3)

जिंदगी है हसीन लेकिन तेरे सपनों के बगैर नहीं हो सके तो लौट
आना मेरे पास
वरना खुद ही लौट आएंगे कभी ना कभी
कुछ तुझे मिलने की बेचैनी ने मुझे छुआ
इसीलिए मुझे लगता है मुझे कुछ तो हुआ
जिंदगी हसीन है लेकिन तेरे सपनों के बगैर नहीं
हो सके तो लौट आना मेरे पास वरना मैं खुद ही लौट आऊंगी तेरे
पास
क्योंकि तेरे प्यार का हुआ है मुझे एहसास
इसीलिए तो है मेरा इतना खास
रहना तू हमेशा मेरे पास
क्योंकि तेरे प्यार का हुआ है मुझे एहसास

(4)

जिंदगी वह किताब है जो खुली रखो तो उसे पढ़ने में आसानी बंद
रखो तो उसे समझने में आसानी यह अपनों की मेहरबानी दी है
अपने जिंदगी की कुर्बानी
वरना हम तो अपनो की महफिल में बेगाने थे
तुझे चाहा बाद में हम अपनो की महफिल में भी दीवाने हो गए
तू तेरी चाहत को मुझे जताने से डर लगता है
क्योंकि तेरी हसरत इतनी हसीन है कि मुझे नजर लग जाने का
इल्जाम किसी के भी सर लगता है

# SHUBHI GUPTA

Ms Shubhi Gupta daughter of Mr.Sanjay Gupta and Mrs.Seema Gupta. She was born on 30 August, 2001 in Kanpur. She is from Pura bazar Ayodhya (U.P).She is a student and writing is her passion just she wants the best feelings that touches her heart to discover more.

# POEM

Walking on a leafy path,as I take my each step forward leaves fly away.
A miniature smile of a child makes me cheerful.
Sinking feather of a bird on my face brings a soft feel to my cheeks.
Cold breeze takes me to the winters.
Oh! I m lost in the world of those flying birds .
Really, it feels awesome to stay in a imaginary world than in a real world,such a peaceful world.
Lifting down with those fondness as I had taken a step forward.
Mood changes with the turning way.
That was a bit of minute which takes me away from the real world.

## (2)

माना की हम मीलों दूर हैं,
फिर भी तेरे नाम में ही एक सुकून है।

तेरे साथ ये रातें भी रंगीन हैं,
ना जाने क्यों ये मन हवाओं के सुर
में ही लीन है।

तेरी बातों पर तो मुझे यकीन है,
मगर ये दिल सच का ही शौकीन है।

## (3)

ज़रा एक बार उस नज़र अंदाज़ को
एक नया अंदाज़ देना।

एक बार उस दिखावे की आंख फोड़ना।

सिर्फ़ एक बार उन अहसासों के नज़रिये से देखना।
क्या पता सच्चाई और चाहत दोनों दिख जाए।

# YUKTA NAWANI

Yukta Nawani is all time learner, an artist by passion and lawyer by profession. A CS aspirant. A fun loving, happy soul who loves to play with words. she is twenty and lives in city Raipur. she believes in enjoying every single moment of her life with zeal and pride. looking for the new possibilites.

# (1)

Add Magical smiles.

She is a bliss,
She is a magical vibe.

She is a fun loving,
And a happy soul.

She loves dancing in the rain,
singing with the birds,
painting with the clouds.

She believes in enjoying,
every single moment of her life,
with zeal and pride.

She is humble enough to win a victory,
calm enough to lose a fight.

She inspires, she motivates, she helps.
She is a perfect example of kindness.

But is she acceptable by the people ?

No,Her kindness judged as a fake act.

She was often called as attention seeker.
People denied her acceptance.
Her existence doubted.
Hatred rises.

Someone asked her,
why she has to pay,

the cost for acting what she is ?

And she replies, "my good deeds
doesn't expect anything in return."

She always believes in one thing,
She says there is something good,
present everywhere in everything.

Some things becomes necessary,
to keep people moving forward.

Let go the negativity,
So it won't hold you longer.

kindness and acceptance,
will lead you to the way,
that is meant to be yours.

She is the vibe,
people crave for.

# KRUTI SUCHAK

Kruti is a spiritual explorer and wanderer in this journey of life. Though fighting with auto immune nervous system disorder and nerve deafness,she lives in grace and joy, turning pain into healing and difficulty into opportunity. She meditates and dives deeper into the inner world. She inspires others to discover the hero and healer within through her spiritual poems and writeups. Thus invokes healing in others. She can be contacted at discovertheherowithin@gmail.com. She can be also contacted on instagram on her page/handle **discovertheherowithin**.

# Poem

I Rise
I rise above the darkness.
I rise above the light.
I rise above death.
I rise above life.
I rise beyond the mountains.
And I rise above the valleys.
Untouched and unpertrubbed by the hardships of life.
I rise above suffering.
I rise above illness.
Graced,adored and blessed by the cosmic light.
I rise above sadness.
I rise above joy and happiness.
Drifted by the cosmic flow.
I rise above fear.
I rise above courage.
Submerged in the cosmic glow.
I rise above success.
I rise above failure.
Untethered by the reality of life.
I rise above fame.
I rise above glory.
Soaked and humbled by divine grace and glory.
I rise above Maya.
I rise above illusion.
Floating in the cosmos.
And laughing at the cosmic play and game of life.

# When the victim becomes the victor

A victim succumbs to situation while a victor always plays the part of a hero actor. A victim holds the hands of vices while a victor holds the hands of virtues. A victim is dependent upon and seeks the support of others whereas a victor is independent and relies on the inner Source. A victim takes an easy road to reach his goals but a victor treads the most difficult path that will lead him towards his spiritual goals.A victim is a zero while a victor is both a zero and hero simultaneously. A victim is a friend of the darkness while a victor is a friend of the light. A victim sinks while a victor floats.The victim says " This is not done" while a victor says "All is well." A victim screams while a victor dreams. A victim cries while a victor always smiles.So, friends, let us become aware of our inner world which will help us to know whether we are victims or victors.If we are victors, it is absolutely great but if we are victims, our effort should be to mould and turn ourselves into victors.As soon as we have negative thoughts, we should immediately check ourselves and not be prone to becoming victims.A victim broods over the past whereas the victor chooses to live in the present. A victim feels he is a loser while a victor feels he is a winner.If we turn our character and personality into that of a victor, then the impossible will become possible, the unfathomable will be fathomable. Then, no vice of anger, greed, lust,attachment or ego shall dare to touch you; only if you become a giver. A victor always says " Yes! I can" and never accepts any kind of negativity as a part of himself. A victor always feels connected with everyone while a victim feels dissociated and isolated from the world.We all can become victors by connecting ourselves to the inner Light and always remaining in tune with the Source; and making ourselves strong with our inner powers and virtues. A victor always stands up and meets the inner war.So, friends, let us all stand up and meet our own inner wars and become victors. Let us all today take an oath of becoming victors in life.Because where the soul opens up its wings and greets life with bravery and courage, then there will be victory.

# Become a Giver

We all want love, peace, joy, happiness and harmony. But we don't check our inner state. If we love our own selves, then only will we be able to transmit that love to others. If we take care of ourselves only then will we be able to take care of others. If we are in a peaceful state, then automatically we will transmit peace to others. If we have compassion for our own selves, then we will automatically have compassion for others. If we are in a state of harmony, then we will automatically be harmonious towards every person, situation and circumstance. You become the solution for you. When you rise to this level, You will be called a giver. So friends, do you want to be a giver or a taker? The choice is ours. If we become a taker, we will suffer. If we become a giver, we will prosper. So who are you? A giver or a taker? Be a giver. Not a taker..

# Poem

Do Not Quit
 Do Not quit
When the storm is being the loudest.
Have the bravery and courage of being the mightiest.
Do Not quit
When the tide of the ocean is the deepest.
Have the hope and faith that your victory is surest.
Do Not quit
When the darkness creeps around you in its fullest.
Have the fire in your consciousness
To keep rising through your inner light to its brightest.
Do not quit
If the cold running down your spine is the chilliest.
Keep raising the wings of fire within your heart
To mould it into the coolest.
Do not quit
When life gives you bolts of suffering.
Have firm faith and belief in " This too shall pass."

# SNEHA DHAMA

Sneha Dhama a twenty years old girl belongs to Khekra Baghpat, Uttar pradesh have lots of dreams and aspirations. Apart being a mbbs student she is a writer who loves to express herself through her writing skills. Ig-sdhama102

# TODAY IS A NEW DAY

Today is a new day,
and a chance to try once more,
to be as good as we are able,
and kinder than before.

Today we pray that we shall behave,
not stamp or squabble, or shout,
but be God's children the way he like,
helping each other out,

We doesn't mean to be selfish,
or to do things that are wrong,
please god help us to leave each other,
and show us how to get along.
MAKE YOURSELF SURROUNDED
IN BETWEEN THE BOUQUET OF NUCLEUS,
BECAUSE YOU HAVE TO SUBSCRIBE
FOR WELLNESS,
WHICH WILL SHOW A GREATNESS IN
YOU,
YOU JUST HAVE TO TRUST YOURSELF
AND YOUR ONE GOOD DEED WILL
MAKE YOU ONE OF THE MOST
FORTUNATE HUMAN BEING AND
YOU WILL BE TREATED AS "DIVINE"
One's goodness is like the rays of light.
However small be the aperture, it
manages to get through lighting up
even the darkest of the rooms..!
With Goodness at heart,
And a Loving soul,
Be Adored by all.

Whether to be good or Bad,
your call
Either to pleasingly Rise,
Or to unfortunately fall.

# DEVIKA SAXENA

Devika saxena is 14yrs old girl Love to write and she is pursuing studies.

## (1)

मुसीबतें भी हस के झेलो
 आगे का सफ़र भी अच्छा लगेगा
कुछ तो होगा तेरे पास जिससे तू ऊपर उठा होगा
कोई तो होगा वो एक मुकाम
जिससे देख कर तू खुश हुआ होगा
कल की मुसीबतों से कुछ नया सीख
तू आगे बड़ा होगा
कोई तो होगा वो एक मुक़ाम
जिससे देख कर तू खुश हुआ होगा
कहीं ना कहीं तूने भी कुछ नया सीखा होगा
कुछ तो होगा तेरे पास जिससे तू ऊपर उठा होगा..

## (2)

एक अलग पहचान होगी मेरी
मुसीबतों में भी मुस्कान होगी मेरी..
पत्थरों पे चलकर मंज़िलों को पाया है हमने
मुसीबतों को सीने से लगा कर जीना सीखा हैं हमने
दुनिया के बदलते चेहरों से जीना सीखा है हमने..

# (3)

खुद ही खुद के बनाए उसूलों पे चलने वालों
मंदिर और मज़ीद में अन्तर करने वालों
हिन्दू और मुस्लिम में फर्क़ करने वालों
कम से कम उस चांद से ही सही कुछ तो सीखो
जो ईद में भी निकालता है और तुम्हारे करवाचौथ को भी..
.

# ANJALI MAURYA

Would like to brief her as aspiring writer. Although not being professional in this field she still loves penning down her thoughts and positive attitude towards the things. All in all will conclude her as writer - - " Being drowned in sea of immense thoughts she found it great to do friendship with words "

# (1)

Goodness is not honey,
That you can buy with money,

Goodness is feeling, abstract,
which gets reflect from your acts,

Goodness sometimes misleads,
If has been done because of greed,

Goodness allows you to lead,
When it comes from your good efforts & deeds,

Being good is art,
Acquiring goodness permanently is really hard,

In changing time of being selfish,
Possess goodness and always remain old yet trending,

External beauty of yours
fades with ages,
But goodness of heart will let you shine spreading smiles on
faces.

# (2)

'अच्छा होना'और 'अच्छाई 'दोनों सुनने में तो एक जैसे ही लगते हैं मगर अन्तर काफी हैं दोनों में। अच्छा होना क्षण मात्र के लिए भी हो सकता है ,जैसे कि वस्तुतः समय में लोगों में देखने को मिल जाता हैं जो स्वार्थ -वश ,लोभ-वश या किसी को हानि पहुँचाने के लिए बनावटी अच्छे होने का ढ़ोग बड़े बढ़िया तरीके से कर लेते हैं। वही दूसरी ओर अच्छाई एक अदृश्य भाव हैं जो सिर्फ अनर्तमन से आता हैं ,और जो हृदय से अच्छा होता हैं उसे किसी भी प्रकार के दिखावें की आवश्यकता नहीं होती   अपितु अच्छाई उसके हाव-भाव ,स्वभाव व कर्मों से स्वयं प्रदर्शित होती हैं।


"मन आपन टटोलिए,
जो मन मैल ना कोई होए,
मन बैर ना कैई होए,
सच्चा मन अच्छा कर चलिए,
ढ़ोग -दिखावा ना कोई होए "

# MUSKAN SACHDEVA

Muskan Sachdeva hails from Basti, uttar Pradesh. She completed studies from St. Basil's and is pursuing Chartered accountant along with bcom from Allahabad university. Writing was just a time pass earlier but then it became her passion. She has been co-authored in 30+ anthologies.

# (1)

To love is from the heart
To hate is from the mind
To smile is from the heart
To cry is from the mind
To be kind is from the heart
To be cruel is from the mind

# PRAGYA VERMA

Pragya Verma hails from Prayagraj, Uttar Pradesh. She is a poetess and a writer. She has done 111+ anthologies, and four international anthologies and currently doing two world record anthologies as a co-author. She is also compiling two anthologies named, "Shades Of Night", "In A Relationship With Success". She has a great interest in making paintings and doing photography. She loves to gain spiritual knowledge and tries to find peace everywhere. You can follow her on Instagram: @wordsofpragya

# Goodness of your Love

The goodness of your love,
The safety in your arms,
Your memories bring all of your charms.

Your pure heart, your true care,
You are someone i don't want to lose I swear.
Sweet, bitter, crazy memories with you,
Is something that will keep me always close to you.

No lies, no cries,
I only want to see your laughter and smiles.
I hate that time when you're not around,
You healed me and recovered my wound.

Crazy moments with happy vibes,
With you my life is full of smiles.
Where to go and whom to find?
In your love, I'm totally blind.

Love is something that brings rejoice,
Everything seems happier when i hear your voice.
My life was full of dark clouds and blues,
You came as a rainbow with lots of hues.

This world is full of broken hearts,
But, you had rejoined my shattered parts.
I love to call you my better half,
With whom my day is full of giggles and laughs.

The day i found you I will never forget,
I want you to me mine in every life i get.
May God, make you mine forever,
I want us to live forever together.

# SAMIKSHA GAUTAM

Samiksha Gautam, a 22 yr old student who aspires to be a writer. She is currently pursuing her studies in ayurveda. ' Heaven's River ' is her debut in an anthology.

## (1)

Like the first rays of the sun
Spread your light with every run,
To achieve the brightest hour,
First burn your power,
So that it gives you the fruit,
Which is the result of your attitude..

## (2)

When the world is asleep
It keeps me awake,
To tell its reality,
That everything which happens here,
Is just to keep you growing,
By God's grace.

## (3)

रात के अंधेरे भी देखा
दिन का उजाला भी देखा,
इस खुश हाल दिल ने बस,
हर जगह उम्मीद का सवेरा ही देखा।

# ARCHISHMAN SATPATHY

Archishman Satpathy, often called the Enthusiast Writer is a young dynamic writer from Deogarh, Odisha. He is presently pursuing B.Tech from IIIT Bhubaneswar. He started writing Quotes and Short Poetries from a young age of 16 and had now made it as his passion. He has contributed as co-author in more than 180 anthologies. He is the author of the book **LAKEEREIN ZINDAGI KE.**

# LET OUR BIRD EXPLORE

Thinking of the hunt for talent within
Let the bird in me explore the Amazon
Let it fly high in the sky of Success
Just because it was once caged tight
We shouldn't always expect that from it
Let the hunger of freedom hunt them all
Happily they will meet up in the horizon
And loudly explain their historic story
Once just try to dive in that oceam stream
And you will find the waves are welcoming
Deep in the core of your gusty little soul
Lets find a way to live extravagant and win
Lets start a new beginning forgetting past
Let the new innings will be the gamechanger
Of the so called enthusiastic life you lived


# WILL WIN OR LEARN

Hey lovely unsuccessful dude standing
What are you watching and thinking?
Are you still in the thought of failure
Or else wants to remember the moment
How you lost and then faces criticism
Am I correct buddy, or something else
Believe me I have a great idea for you
From where you left, start thinking from there
Just idealising the process or proceedings
May give you a chance to think about
You have to try again and that too now
From where you left, start trying from there
Definitely you will learn something more
And may succeed in this attempt dude

# TRY TILL YOUR DOOM

Never ever I thought of the criticism
Just believes the fact everytime that
Either you will win or learn something
Tried to give off but thanks conscience
Shall I try once again is my question and
Everytime I get the answer of "YES"
Just because I was close to win last time
I can never thought of giving off also
Trying to synchronise my soul into fate
Now I am going to try my luck with sound
Whatever the result will be, can't break me
If possible I will try till the doom and gloom
Lets fly in the high sky of life happily ever
And achieve the horizon into our pockets


# GOODNESS OF THE SELF

Do your confidence on yourself
Slowly and deeply became extinct
Then just think of your existence here
There must be any purpose of yours
Just have faith and love on yourself
Self love is the best weapon
That a sweet soul is searching
We must acknowledge the happenings
That turns to be gamechangers of our life
We often cursed the self within
Crying and depriving from outfits
Totally ignoring our hidden heroics
Which will one day change the critics

# AGAM SACHDEVA

She is an extremely talented girl with a very beautiful mind. She writes so well at such a young age. Though, she is just 14 years old but still is adored by many people. She has been a part of many anthologies earlier and has made her parents proud. She is a beautiful creation of God.

# GOODNESS

Goodness lies in daily details,
In a simple delights,
It is all that is calm,
With soft edges and
It is also relaxing arms.
It is being happy
And making others smile.
It is being YOU.

# GOODNESS

Going to help the poor,
Play, dance and feed your hunger
It is still helping
And ignoring your ego
It is still being a kid,
And dance out your soul,
It is being kind,
Not just to others,
But,
Yourself too

# GOODNESS

Goodness for you,
Is in being happy,
Always keep smiling.
It is having a pride feeling.
It is you being you.
It is penning down your thoughts.
And helping yourself relive.

# GOODNESS

Goodness is giving someone a reason to live,
It is giving someone a season to enjoy.
It is making their day,
It is making them dance and giving them butterflies.

# NARENDRA KUMAR RAYAKWAR

He is Narendra Rayakwar(Software Engineer) from Jhansi Utter Pradesh. His father Mr. Deendayal Rayakwar is a senior inspector in fisheries department and his mother Draupadi Devi Rayakwar is a home maker. He has completed m.tech in computer science. His dream is become a businessman for help to needy or poor person. He is a good motivator, He was inspired by his father. He loves to make MOTIVATIONAL short videos and his Facebook page is NK MOTIVATIONAL. He is a Youtuber and his YouTube channel is NK technical Narendra Kumar Rayakwar. His favourite line is "A person is not poor, he is poor only by mind". Instagram ID :- narendrag278

# मुहब्बत

मुहब्बत का मतलब् प्यार, प्रेम, लगाव जो किसी व्यक्ति, बस्तु या जगह से होता है । जब आप अपना समय किसी दूसरे इंसान के लिए बरबाद करने लगते हैं तो समझ जाइये कि आप उस इंसान से प्यार करने लगे हैं । लेकिन मेरा मानना है कि यदि आप किसी से बेइन्तहा मुहब्बत करते हैं तो आप उसके लिए कुछ भी करने को तैयार हो जायेंगे । और आप भी यही सोचते हैं कि जितना प्यार मैं करता हूँ उतना ही प्यार मुझे भी मिलेगा । मैं जो चाहूँ बो मुझे मिलेगा, जैसा बोलूंगा बैसा ही होगा, तो आप 100% गलत हैं ।क्योंकि प्यार, मुहब्बत या दोस्ती में आप कुछ भी करने को तैयार हो जायेंगे लेकिन उसके बदले में जो भी उम्मीद रखते हैं उसमें आपका मतलब छुपा होता है, और जहाँ मतलब होता है, वहां प्यार, मुहब्बत नहीं और जहाँ प्यार होता है वहां कोई मतलब नहीं होता, सिर्फ प्यार होता है सिर्फ प्यार ।

लेकिन मेरे प्यारे मित्रो आप प्यार किससे करते हैं, उसे जो आपको अपना बनाने के लिये अपने माता-पिता, भाई-बहन, परिवार सभी को त्याग देना चाहता है, यानी कि आप उसे प्यार करते हैं। आप यह नहीं जानते कि जिसने आपको बचपन से ही नहीं बल्कि जब आप माँ की कोख से भी बाहर नहीं निकले थे तब से प्यार किया और आज अपनी जान से भी ज्यादा प्यार करते हैं, बो माता-पिता आपको अपनी जिंदगी, अपनी इज्जत मानते हैं । आज आपने किसी गैर इंसान के छोटे से दिखावटी प्यार को सच्चा प्यार समझ लिया और अपने माता-पिता जीवन दाता उनको आपने एक ही झटके में पराया कर दिया । उनकी इज्जत को मानो बाजार में नीलाम कर दिया । मेरे प्यारे मित्रो एक तुच्छ से प्यार करने वाले दिखावटी, मतलबी इंसान के लिए आपने अपने भगवान रूपी माता-पिता के दिल को दुखी करने की कोशिश की है । जिसने आपको जीवन दिया फिर चलना सिखाया और जीवन की राह पर चलना सिखाया, जिंदगी की सारी खुशियाँ दी । आपको ऐसे माता-पिता को दुखी करने का अधिकार किसने दिया । आप एक बार अपने माता-पिता की बात को दिल से महसूस करने की कोशिश करके तो देखिए, आपको पता चल जायेगा कि दुनिया में आपका ऐसा कोई मित्र नहीं होगा जो माता-पिता के जैसे आपको प्यार कर सके। आपके प्यार करने वाले, आपके ऊपर मर-मिटने वाले दिखावटी लोग बहुत मिलेंगे लेकिन जीवन

भर साथ देने वाला, साथ जीने वाला, आपको जीवन के सही मायने बताने वाला जीवनसाथी बहुत ही नसीब वालों को मिलता है । आप कभी अपने माता-पिता को दुखी ना करें, आप अपने माता-पिता की आँखों के तारे हैं ।

# सफलता

जीवन की राह पर चलकर आप अपने सपने को पूरा करने के लिए मेहनत इतनी करें कि सफलता खुद ही चलकर आपके कदम चूमेगी । मेरे प्यारे मित्रो आप अपने सपनों से प्यार करना सीखें और दिन-रात अपने लक्ष्य को प्राप्त करने के लिए मेहनत करते रहे। लोग कहते हैं जब आप सोते हैं तब सपने आते हैं, लेकिन मेरा मानना है कि सपने बो होते हैं जिससे आपकी रातों की नींद उड़ गई हो । आप अपना दिल व दिमाग अपनी शिक्षा पूरी करने, अपने सपने को पूरा करने में लगा दो। एक दिन बो आयेगा जिस दिन आप जरुर सफल होंगे और आपकी सफलता के उदाहरण लोग अपने बच्चों को बतायेंगे । सफल वही होता है जो इंसान अपने साथ-साथ अपने माता-पिता और परिजनों को भी खुश रखे, लेकिन यदि आप एक सफल इंसान नहीं है और आप सफल होना चाहते हैं तो समझ जाइये कि आपको उस समय सभी से दूर रहना पडेगा और उस बक्त में बहुत से अपने लोग आपसे खफा हो जायेगे । आप उनके चक्कर में अपने लक्ष्य को मत भूलियेगा क्योकि जिस दिन आप सफल हो जायेगे उस दिन सारे रिश्ते-नाते आपके साथ होंगे । आपकी सफलता की तारीफ करेंगे और सभी गिले-सिकबो को भूल जायेंगे

# जीवन

जिस दिन आप अपने जीवन जो जीना सीख जाओगे उस दिन जिंदगी लंबी नहीं बड़ी जीने की बात करोगे । खुद के लिए तो सभी जीते हैं, कभी दूसरे के लिए जीना तो सीखें। दिल को बहुत सुकून मिलेगा ।

लोग हमेशा अपने माता-पिता, अपने बीवी-बच्चों और परिवार के लिए ही मेहनत करते हैं, एक बार बिना स्वार्थ के किसी गरीब का सहारा बन के तो देखिए, जिंदगी को जीने का मजा ही बदल जायेगा ।

उस खुदा, उस भगवान का शुकिया अदा करो कि आप दोनों बक्त का भोजन भर पेट करते हैं, यदि आप भी इस काबिल है कि किसी गरीब की भूख मिटा सके तो जरुर उनके भूखे पेट का सहारा बने, उनकी मदद करें। ऐसा करने से आप भगवान तो नहीं बन सकते लेकिन गरीबों के मसीहा जरुर कहलाये जाओगे ।

भगवान भी आपका सहयोग करेंगे और आपको इस काम के लिए धन्यवाद कहेंगे ।

आज यदि आप किसी की मदद करते हैं तो बो परम पिता परमेश्वर उसी बक्त आपकी मदद के लिए किसी न किसी को जरुर पैदा कर देता है, लेकिन आप जिसकी मदद करते हैं, आप उससे मदद की उम्मीद नहीं करना ।

मैं नरेन्द्र आपसे कहना चाहता हूँ कि यदि आप किसी की मदद नहीं कर सकते हैं तो कोई बात नहीं परंतु कभी किसी का बुरा मत करना ।

किसी ने सच ही कहा है कि "जियो और जीने दो"

अंत में बस कहूँगा कि आप सभी के लिए अच्छे बने और जग में अपना नाम रोशन करें ।

# SADHWIKA SUMA

A writer by heart, "Sadhwika suma from Nizamabad Telangana". Daughter of "Holapu Sudharshan and Vani". Beginner with an Instagram page. 19 years old girl who is a daydreamer which dreams won't let her sleep. She writes like she owns the beautiful things in the Universe. She writes her thoughts on very tiny things which happen in her daily routine. She lives happily with a dream to become an author someday. A strong believer in the love, hope, universe and it's magic. Her thoughts as words give her anonymous peace. She put her soul in her words. Many teenagers can feel the power of love and pain in her words. From normal quotes, writer at 17 to a become a poetess she proved herself as a writer. Her wings spread widely, and ink spills from the aorta of her heart. Writing makes her complete. She can pen with no boundaries… It took 19 years to realize her love towards the dam full of words in her heart, ready for the gates to be opened in the form of ink in her pen when finally destined herself to be a writer and a poet. And she had dream to inspire millions of people through her stories and poems. To fall in love with her writings visit Instagram:- @Sadhwika_writings To fall in love with her stories visit WordPress:- www.sadhwikasuma.wordpress.com

# Money Can't Buy Goodness

do not follow me
there is a curse
for all good people
who arrive always at
the end
with nothing
but i never regret
this thing
i am good i was
good and that is
enough for me
for in this goodness
nothing pleases me
except the goodness itself
look at me
do not even me
for i am good for goodness
sake
there is no money in it
i tell you
but what all i have
is what
money cannot buy
money talks
but i have arrived
at this point
when it is not
worth my time anymore
money talks
and i am not listening
at all
virtue is as silent
as the still water

it has the voice of
winds
the dance of leaves
amidst the
morning light

## Goodness Of People

There is goodness in small and big,
Whether this is small or big this tells,
Every work needs ethics and values,

Life designed in such way gets success.
Goodness blooms and goodness shines,
With beautiful personality and joy,
Having trust within life and dignity,
Every little success comes to give joy.

Material things are in small goodness,
All perishable achievements lie here,
Temporary things we cannot say broad,
Big goodness comes from spiritual way.

Every spiritual value shows path of light,
This makes human beings tender and polite,
Person does not become egoistic and rude,
His/Her goodness of action pleases others.

# Good Belongs To You

So, Celebrate It By Yourself"

I CELEBRATE myself;
And what I assume
you shall assume;
For every atom belonging to me,
as good belongs to you.

I loafe and invite my Soul;
I lean and loafe at my ease,
observing a spear of summer grass.

Houses and rooms are full of perfumes the shelves
are crowded with perfumes;
I breathe the fragrance myself,
and know it and like it;
The distillation would
intoxicate me also,
but I shall not let it.

The atmosphere is not
a perfume it has no taste
of the distillation it is odorless;
It is for my mouth
forever I am in love with it;

I will go to the bank
by the wood,
and become undisguised and naked;
I am mad for it to be in contact with me.

# Good Is In You

Good is a four letter word,
More powerful than sword;
Forming the life's core-
Without which life is sore;

Bad is a word with letter three,
Built upon the vice tree;
Hatching evils in minds free,
Stop it before it kills thee;

In night's darkness hunts the Owl,
Like the vices from the heart of any soul,
As in the day the rose fragrance flows,
Goodness spreads happiness in full bowl;

# PRIYANKA VARMA

She is Priyanka Varma studying Master's of Pharmacy from Visakhapatnam. She is a National and Central Zonal Sports Player along with being a Classical Dancer and an Artist. Along with these, She is also a poetess fond of writing her thoughts. she believes that "The true beauty is reflected in the soul."

# COLOURS OF LIFE

A Rainbow is one of the most fascinating and captivating spectacles, that one can ever witness. Everyone loves the sight of a rainbow in a partially cloudy sky.

So, what is it that makes it so spectacular..?

Is it the shape..?

Is it the size..?

Is it the array of distinct colours, so beautifully merged together..? Or,

Is it the rainbow's ephemeral nature that endears it to us..?

All the factors cumulatively do appeal to us. However, it is the wide array of distinct colours that gives a rainbow it's due recognition. Would a single colour strip on the sky, enthral us as much as a rainbow does..?

A Band of Red…or

A Ribbon of Blue … or

A Strip of Green….or

A Shred of your Favourite Colour….No!

So is Life..!

Our lives are filled with Colours from the start -

RED is the Love, comes from HEART

BLUE is the Sadness, drips from  EYES

BLACK is the Evil, makes us a LIAR

GREEN is the Shades of JEALOUSY and RAGE

GREY is the Hair, comes with OLD AGE

PURPLE is the Mood, most MIS-UNDERSTOOD

But WHITE is the colour, makes us FEEL GOOD

But especially White, so hold on to it tight.

LIFE is full of meaningful and different colours, makes us to move in every path atleast once in OUR LIFE.

Life assumes meaning as well as proportion vide the myriad situations it encounters. Situations being inextricably interwoven into the fabric of life, meet perception, to unleash a wide range of emotions like Joy, Happiness, Hope,

Sadness, Despair, Anger, Surprise etc. These constitute the 'COLOURS OF LIFE' that all of us remain immersed in, throughout our lives.

So Paint the rest of the days with the Best colours. LIVE a LIFE that MATTERS.

# A BEAUTIFUL SOUL

When people look at my heart,
They may find beauty,
They may say I am beautiful because of my gentle spirit,
They may say I am beautiful because of my kindness,
They may say I am beautiful because of my bravery and fearlessness,
They may say I am beautiful because of my joyful smile,
But the beauty is not defined by facial mode, but by a beautiful soul.
A beautiful soul is made from celestial light.
Your mirror image may some day fade,
But the soul you behold will be heavenly made.
The true beauty is reflected in the soul..!!

# GANESH SADASHIV PATIL

This Is Ganesh Sadashiv Patil.He Is The Student Of UG In Field Of Pharmacy.He Has Writer And Poet Who Writes 100+ Poetry In Hindi And Marathi Languages.He Loves To Write On Love,Humanity, Motivation And Social Themes.He loves to write down his feelings, his thoughts on various topics which makes him a writer of one his own kind.

# छिपा हुआ अंधेरा

ना जाने वो सूरज छुपा हुआ है अंधेरेसे कब निकलेगा ये ना पता है
नये उमंग से भरी रोशनी के संग वो निकलेगा यही मन में आशा है
छुपी हुई बुराइयो को जड से उखाडकर उन्हे ना हमे बढावा देना है

छिपे हुए इस अंधेरेमें रोशनी लाकर झगमघाहट हमे यहा फैलानी है

छुपकर किये जा रहे बुरे कामो को अच्छाई के कर्म से नष्ट करना है

हर एक रहे यहा नेक और नम्रता से हमे ना बैर किसीमे होने देना है

छिपे हुए झूठ और स्वार्थी विचारोको अपने इस मनसे निकाल देने है

रास्ता अपनाना है सत्यता और प्रेम का इसी राह पर चलते जाना है

आज आवो संगमें सारे एकत्रित यहा करेंगे मिलकर संकल्प सारे है
मदत करेंगे हम सबकी यहा मिलकर ये शपथ हम आज सब लेते है

# मुझे लिखना पसंद है क्योंकि

ना जाने कौनसा जुनून है मुझमे जो में इस तरह शब्दो को बया करता हूं

लिखने की ये आदत लग गयी है ऐसी की में कलम के बिना ना रेहता हूं

सुना है बोलणे से ज्यादा यहा सबको पढकर सब कुछ समजमें आता है

बात ये आयी दिमाग में जब मेरे ये कलम और कागज अब साथ होता है

लिखने का जुनून है मुझमे ऐसा की लिखानही मेरे शब्दोको बया करते है

यही लिखान अब बन गया है साथ मेरा आज पेहचान जुडी मेरी उससे है

आदत अब जो पड गयी है मुझे इसकी ऐसे की हुआ है मुझे कोई नशा है

इस नशे में ही रहेंगे हम जीवनभर इसमे डूब जाने को भी अब हम तयार है

लिखना है पसंद मुझे इस जीवन में क्योकी वो मेरी चाहत अब बन गयी है

ये चाहत ऐसी हि बरकरार रहेगी जीवन में कमी न इसकी यहा ना होनी है

# अच्छाई

किया हो बुरा हमारा किसिने जिंदगी में ना उसके बर्ताव पर नाराज होईए

जाना तो है एक दिन हमेभी यहासे बात थोडी अपनोसे आप कर लिजीए

कडवाहट भरी हो अगर मन में अपने तो ना उसे कभीभी आप यु जताईए

बदल दिजिये यहा मिठे बोलसे सबका मन अपने आप को ना दुःख दिजीए

प्यार से हि तो बढते है रिशते यहा ऐसेही डोर उनकी भी बंधती जाती है

इस डोर का ना तुटणे दिजीए जीवन में कभी अपनो को संग लाकर रखीए

अच्छाई को ये दुनिया सदा याद रखती है बुराई की तो बदनामी हि होती है

हम रहे याद यहा सबको जीवन में काम कुछ ऐसा जिंदगी में करके जाईए

नम्रता से रेहकर जीवन में यहा हमे सबको साथ लेकर आगे बढते जाना है

ना हो कोई भी व्यवहार से रुठा हमारे ऐसा ना काम कोई हमे यहा करना है

# जीवन

जीवन का बस एक यही उद्देश है सबको यहा हमे खुश रखना है
कोई ना हो मायूस यहापर हमसे ना किसीओ करना मायूस हमे है
सुख हर एक को हमे देना है दुःख ना किसिके जीवन में लाना है
हर एक को मिले यहा खुशी बस इसी बात पर हमे गौर करना है
आचरण ये हमारा अच्छा रखना है ना किसिसे हमे बेहस करना है
योग्यअयोग्य का ध्यान रखकर हमे आगे मंजिल पर बढते जाना है
स्वार्थ से भरे मन को हमें काबू में रखना है ना इसे बिछडणे देना है
निस्वार्थी मन से कर के सेवा यहा हमे जिंदगी में बस खुश रेहना है
नफरते ना यहा हमे बढने देनी है प्यार की भाषा को हि सिखलाना है
हरएक रहे संग मिलकर यहा बस इसी बात पर हमे ध्यान रखना है

# SAHINA GHUGHA

Sahina Ghugha is 20 year old b.com student at Saurashtra university Rajkot. She is from Jamnagar city of Gujarat. She is state level winner in poetry competition 2017. She is Co-author of 15+ anthologies. She is an amazing writer and poet and she wants do something for society through her pen. Insta ID:- Itz_Sahina_write

# अच्छाई

मौजूदगी अच्छाई की ज़हेन में जो रखता है
अल्लाह उस बंदे को खुशियां देता है।

राग द्वेष से हो परे जो, हो बंदगी में मशगूल
खुदा भी ऐसे मुरीद की खैरियत पूछता है।

हो भलाई की नीति दिल में दूसरे लोगों के लिए
भगवान भी खुश हो कर उसका खयाल रखता है।

जिसने भला चाहा दूजे का, हुआ भला उसका भी
कुदरत अपनी महरबानी हर बंदे को बख्शता है।

रखिए ना दिल में बुराई किसी के लिए कभी भी
ईश्वर हमेशा सच्चे और अच्छे लोगो की सुनता है।

होती कुबूल है दुवाएं भी ऐसी शर्त से जनाब
परमात्मा दूसरों के लिए कुछ मांगो तो देता है।

है वो जानता सबके राज़, जाने सबके कर्म वो
विधाता है वो, सबके नसीब लिखता पहचानता है।

भलाई की ज्योत जली रहे, मददगार बनो किसी के
परमेश्वर तुम में दिखने लगे, वो हर जगह बसता है।

दिल में चाहो भला किसी का, सोचो ना कभी बुरा
प्रभु होंगे प्रभावित तुमसे, वो सब पे ध्यान देता है ।

है चलाता जगत वो, तुम्हारी अच्छाई के सहारे ही
जगदीश है वो पर ध्यान किसी का तुमको रखना है।

# ISHRAT SABOON

Ishrat saboon,from j&k,a passionate writer and a student with classical dreams and vivid wings.she has worked as a co-author in so many anthologies.she loves to pen her feelings she is an introvert but her pen makes her extrovert .she started writing as a time pass but mean time she enjoyed this.she deeply believe that the depth of her heart and the nib of her pen are soulfully connected Her Instagram id:ishratsaboon11 Email id: ishratsboon@gmail.com

# Goodness

Softly my fears whispered invisible lies,
my heart is a Keeper of those wrapped truths,
But,
It melted in the waves
You intended me to drown in

# Goodness in her

She quietly lived
In the scarred spin,
An off hand amble ,with a fractured soul
taken handily

# RAHEJA SUMIT

A Writer with beauty behind words. A teacher for smiles , development inspite trouble & struggle. A forever learner (student) from heart (HSC - Arts / Humanities) from motherland India, Maharashtra - Ulhasnagar. Believes in working hard , staying kind,Works from heart.

# POEM

Away from worldly desires a beautiful smile of goodness lie
!
Away from worldly lies crying with tears but firm truth lie !
This goodness - a symbol of truth lies
Goodness that let all sorrows fly
Goodness which with now or then but once the world stands
by
Goodness with which numerous struggles and simplicity both
attach ,
One as treasure and one as pleasure stay ..
Some take this goodness till hairs get gray
Some just for good ones in mind stay
Some kill it because of cruel world ...
I hope happiness and well being knock their doors or they
may

# KAREENA VERMA

She is kareena verma The Daughter of Mr.Kehru verma & Mrs.Rajeshwari verma . She is a computer science student and currently pursuing the bachelor of application And she is very passionate in writing and co- author of many anthologies and as well as many international Anthologies too. In this world only her pen & diary is the best friend to penned her pain in the blank pages of life Diary . And same as her name Kareena delineate alike her name , sanguine with her soul, pure with her heart , innocent with her straightforward thoughtful perceptions! For her Rectitude within her is everything & nothing is above than Viracity with our nation , she wants only to flame alike terracotta Diya, for one day she'll spread the happiness of lights as the most bright star in the sky of someone home and just wanna to spread love of humanity every where !!

# *THE GOODNESS IN YOU*

I already met my inner Goddess,
I call her "Wild Woman"!

Sometimes she knew, she could become weak
but she had the choice to be at the peak.

Sometimes she knew,she could rest
But she had the choice to be the become best.

Sometimes she knew,she could hide threatened feelings,
but she had choice To fight what's  inside it.

Sometimes she knew close all the obstacles doors
but she had choice explore the her profligate wild woman.

Sometimes she knew ,she could withstand the Storm
but she had the choice to be the Storm.

Choose your standards wisely,
And she knew she could be the
survivor but
she had the choice to be the warrior.

She is the warrior, this is her choice
Because she can't be your alike optional subject bin your life

,

You can't be compared you from the others,
She is unique in her every way of life ,

She is the a fighter , who is Fighting for her dreams ,
She is the a daughter, a mother and a wife ,

She is the one , who is creating whole world of yours ,
And She is the Goodness in you always ,
Always respect a woman , who is your own world of life &
others too

This writeups only for a strong woman!

# *GOODNESS OF THE NEW ME*

Who am I........
A fallen poor person
With a broken emotion
My soul is calling, hey listen

Let's try our new version
With a new energy
Breaking down my inner lethargy
Again I started with a smile
For walking thousands of mile

Leaving my past history
Trying to write a new mystery
Capturing my inner glory
Understood, the earth is so merry

With these goodness I appear now
Unable to catch up heart somehow
With a thirst soul for Success thriving
Going to strive hard for thirst of chaos


With a clear mind and heart
I moved for the second part
Putting calmness in my cart
From the god's beautiful mart.

# SHWETA AGNIHOTRI

Shweta Agnihotri is a learner"(she likes to learn every day something new and that makes her writing more efficient. She likes to find new words, and love to put that words in her writing.
She  want to learn more till the end of her life because writing is very broad and huge world. It gives you all the time, you have taken one, it gives you new one. She  has unique thinking and skill to create in her words towards her writing. and she thinks that, all the writers are different than the other because only writer can make water drop romantic, meaningful, or tear of nature because writer has different ways to see the world.)

# माँ

वो आहटें, वो हँसीं
वो नाकाम नाराजगी
वो प्यारी सी कोशिशें
वो तुम्हारा मुसकुराना
वो मेरा ख्याल रखना
वो मुझे समझाना
सब याद रहता है मुझे
हाँ भूल जाती हुँ अक्सर चीजों को बड़ा
मगर वो तुम्हारा मुसकुराता चेहरा
याद रहता है मुझे
हाँ सब याद रहता है मुझे।

# उम्मीद

बातों को, जज़बातों को
कहकर उन्हें आजाद कर देना होगा,
जो हो चुका उन बातों को भुला देना होगा,
अपनों को सब बता देना होगा,
मुश्किलों को आसान कर देना होगा,
अतीत को पिछे छोड़ देना होगा,
आने वाले कल को अपना कर देना होगा,
मंजिल की तरफ खुद को मोड़ देना होगा,
पनाह लिए गमों को रुख़सत कर देना होगा,
खुशियों की बंजर ज़मीं पर
आस का फूल खिला देना होगा,
अब फासला हो चाहे जितना
बिना थके, बिना रुके अब आगे बढ़ते हुए
जिन्दगी को दूसरा मौका देना होगा।

# एहसास

राहों से मंजिल कोई जुदा नहीं
हौसलों से बुलंद कोई जज्बा नहीं
इरादों से ऊंचा कोई आसमां नहीं
दर्द से गहरा कोई समंदर नहीं
कोशिशों से बेहतर कोई जीत नहीं
मायूसी से बढ़ा कोई जख्म नहीं
तमन्नाओं से अलग कोई इच्छा नहीं
तारीफों से सच्ची कोई प्रेरणा नहीं
झूठ से बुरी कोई तकलीफ नहीं
ईमान से बेहतर कोई इबादत नहीं
करने से ज्यादा कोई काम नहीं
कदमों से आगे कोई रास्ता नहीं
यकीं से खूबसूरत कोई वादा नहीं
तो रख यकीं खुद पर फिर
तुझसे अच्छा कोई इंसान नहीं।

# अजनबी

चल रही है सांस एक तरफ
एक तरफ धड़कन रूक रही।
क्या प्यार है ये क्या जिन्दगानी है,
चलते चलते मिले ख्वाबों में
 इक इशारे से उसके पीछे दौड़ पड़ी,
क्या जानती थी कि वो एक सपना है या सच
पर उसके साथ बहुत खुश मैं रहने लगी,
वो आया सपने में तो सोने का ख्याल आ जाता है
वो चला ना जाए इस डर से उठने का मन नहीं करता,
साँसे चल रही लेकिन धड़कन रूक रही,
क्या प्यार है ये क्या जिन्दगानी है
चल रही है सांस एक तरफ
एक तरफ धड़कन रूक रही।

# PRINCY CAROL GONSALVES

Princy is a writer from Quepem, Goa. Currently studying in 2nd year. Besides a writer she is also an artist who loves to do beautiful paintings and artistic creative things.The newspapers in her state gave voice to her words and published her write-ups numerous times. She shares her write-ups on Instagram handle @shades_of_emotions_ She is a introvert yet she loves to express herself in her write-ups.

# Charity and Generosity

If you feel anybody needs help, don't hesitate to serve,
spend your precious time with your grandparents, gift them
some love and care they deserve.

Give the poor and weak's but don't expect from them that
you will seek,
No matter in which religion, caste or creed they belong
don't differentiate nor expect from them in return

Be approachable for the ones who are in need,
Be like the water which nourishes the seed
Instead of being selfish and filled with greed
Help others to proceed

Donate without announcing
Try to be kind, generous and acknowledging
keep your ego aside at the end we just dust,
Dust that will fade away one day

Charity starts with you, it starts from your every thought,
 learn to forgive others mistakes as well as learn to share and
give.

# Goodness like Sunshine

Be the sun which spreads sunshine,
Be that important heart beat that saves a lifeline

When life throws you in the dark,
Instead of losing hope you should embark

When dark clouds try to overtake,
Rebuild yourself even if it costs you, a short break.

Choice is yours whether you wish to shine alone during the day, to rule the throne
Or want to be like tough stones which are worthy yet unknown

Many curse and hate the sun for shinning bright in summers
Many invites and long to feel the warmth in monsoons as well as winters

Every one is unique as each one have their own importance
There's a need for you to realize others worth in their presence.

# I wish to breath in a world like this

I wish to breath in a world like this
Where people live happily in equality
Where there are No religions, neither castes, nor differences,
All that matters in this world, is goodness and humanity
Here creepy people don't exist.

I wish to breath in a world like this,
Where the world encourages you to do good to others,
Where nobody knows to criticize
Neither to distinguish nor to compare
As kindness and love runs in their veins

I wish to breath in a world like this
a world which doesn't know to spread hatred,
neither to take revenge nor to discriminate
People from here know to forgive and
This world is exactly the opposite of the world wherein I live

# Goodness

In this world so cruel be someone who spreads goodness,
Forget partiality and bias

Don't just be kind to words,
Wearing different masks like wizards

Think and do good deeds,
You will be a superman in someone's life indeed

Having a kind heart is a blessing but at times it feels like a
curse
as you aren't able to make them taste their own selfishness.

Still do good to others
As you are rare and one in lots
not in aughts.

Remember that a kind heart with a pure soul is a bit rare
But a kind face with an evil mind is found everywhere.

# ALIYA SIDDIQUA

An alluring girl , **Aliya siddiqua** is pursuing 12th standard bipc .She is from Hyderabad Telangana, she is a co-author of 4 books. she write the poetry more and quick quotes and she know very well singing  and dancing quite. she is interested in modelling or acting , she is quite multi-talented. she is interested in her own book to write to express her feelings curious in other professionals, so join a fashion designer classes ,
Email : princessaliyasiddiqua@gmail.com

# WATERS ARE THE WAYS

River are heaven ,
Stream like a sky ,
The river reflects the  reflection ,
And the flow ,
Flow will run ,
The fresh water streams ,
the beauty of the river is natural ,
Seems not to be harm ,
But the useful for ,
The road which sweeps you gently,
River take us , where the wish of the flow
Not another but the river ,
River are the heaven .
Rivers will go straight like a time ,
And it will never be reverse ,
The past never be reverse,
Not the future ,
Rivers are heaven ,
It's disappearance will make us die ,
It's appearance will make us bright ,
And precious time, like a river are absolutely one .

Whether changes , but not the river ,
Colours appears on rainbow, but not in the river ,
River is pure form ,
And the river like a heaven .
Pulling over a door ,
And pushing over the world,
And the river water waves take you to the whole world,
The flow goes where it goes,
On the ground, the fine and purest form of the things is water
,
As river the heaven.

# AISHWARYA UMASHANKAR

An enthusiastic person with a positive spirit towards everything. Hailing from Tamilnadu with a vision to experience, enjoy and succeed in every task taken. Lives with a moto 'Short life with a big world to enjoy. Hence Never accept anything low'. Rising with love for world and nature and blooming in the form of poetries at her instagram handle __uv_says.Here's the one from the bottom of her heart to reiterate the beauty of our birth, the good heart and make readers believe in goodness and a better tomorrow.May this bring in better sunshine to the readers' life and kindle positivity.

# Incarnation of goodness

To be born as a human
And to share feelings of love,mercy and courtesy
is the greatest privilege of our birth.
With a heart that weeps
and a mind that cares
is where goodness takes birth !
No matter how hard it is to leap
towards the next step that is far
never stop preaching your goodness!
Let the goodness that you grow in your soul
Creep and climb completely in your body
and get scattered around you.
The privileged one who gets even a little shadow
of yours finds peace in and around.
You be an abode of good will and spirit !
and make someone believe in a better tomorrow.
Everything that hinders your path
And everything that tears you
Shall bend at your goodness
And mend you even better.
You be an "**Incarnation of Goodness!**

# MOHANAPRIYA.K

Co-author Mohanapriya.K is a good writer from Tamilnadu, India. She has completed her Bachelor's degree in Engineering stream. She has been a writer for one year as her passion. She wants to be a best compiler and curator in future. She will try to express what comes to her mind through her words as it is. For her writing is a great art. The art of giving pleasure to the mind and helping to forget the worries in the mind. She is very happy to undertake such noble art. Yet she sincerely hope that this writing journey of her will continue as sweetly as it is now and will bring her many successes. She also loves singing, gardening and drawing. I.G : @colours_honey_official E-mail : doraa.kutty@gmail.com

# The goodness of our life is that we live happily in this world

My desire is to always be happy.

The happiness that surrounds us is also important.

More important than that is the happiness that is within us.

Always want to live happily smiling.

Then there is a meaning in our lives.

There is no substitute for the joys of the festive season.

We may change over time but the happiness within us will remain the same.

So we have to learn to live with laughter without forgetting laughter in any situation.

No one has the right to prevent us from expressing our views.

But in some situations some people push us into this situation.

What we need to make clear to them is that we are not mentally weak.

# Make sure you always have goodness in you

I'm more confident in the beliefs I have!
She is never bored of trusting me!
The reason is the disappointments I have received from others.
Living for others is life!
But not living forever for us is definitely not life for us!
Confidence in what we do will make us successful in it.
Trust us!
Let's taste the fruits of a lot of success!
There is no limit to true love and there is no rule for unconditional love.
The privilege of our life is to live with the person with whom we desire to live and to spend our entire life with him.

# Living with smile is also goodness

No matter how many difficulties in your life you should not lose your laughter for it.
Because not laughing means no problem is going to go right.
But if we handle our problems with a smile and fight, there is a lot of chance that it will get better.
We do not know when or what will happen in our life.
The next minute is a life of uncertainty.
So learn to live the life you live in peace and happiness.
You are the top most priority for you.
Don't lose yourself for anyone.
Anyone can change anyway but the relationship between you and you will never change.
Just accept yourself.

# There is a lot of goodness in loving others

The love we show to others should be our own volition and we should not allow others to interfere too much in that desire.

We should not expect the same love that we pay to be forced on us by the person we love.

Maybe if we look forward to doing so sometimes only one disappointment overwhelms us.

Love can have control but control alone should not be love.

The most important thing is to live with love in love and if you forget it then that love will be gone.

We will spend our precious time with the people we love the most.

We will give unconditional love and live happily.

What a beautiful feeling love is!

Love wins or loses but it is always filled with a feeling of beauty in the mind.

Because lovers can lose but love never fails.

# M.HASEEBUNISSA

M. Haseebunissa is a young, aspiring and a vibrant leader holding sound knowledge in theoretical and practical aspects of counselling. She holds a Masters in Applied Psychology and is currently pursuing her Master of Philosophy in Counselling. She is a certified NLP Practitioner. She loves to write and believes in the magic of words to transform lives. She finds solace in writing. Her work at various domains involves promoting optimal mental health.

# 'Coz why not?'

Let's teach each other
The art of loving;
For too many pure souls crave
Unconditional love.

Let's teach each other
How those appreciations,
And little acts of kindness
Goes a long way.

Let's teach each other
The importance of staying connected;
That dropping by, to meet somebody
Is always greater than dropping million texts.

Let's teach other
How real hugs feel like;
Nah! Not those polite or one way hugs;
The one that wards off pain and gives solace.

Let's teach other
That it's okay to fail,
And how it's not okay
To not try.

Let's teach each other
That we have each other's back
In both the crests and troughs
Of life!

Let's teach other
That's It's not okay
To compromise on the self respect

No matter what

Let's teach other
That it's okay to cry;
And weep;
And take a break whenever it feels like it.

Let's teach each other
To teach each other goodness,
For that alone lasts.
Let's teach each other.

# PRASAD BABU GALLA

Prasad Babu Galla is born and brought up in Visakhapatnam, Andhra Pradesh. He is a passionate co-author and compiler of anthologies. He is more into writing love and inspirational quotes and poems. You can pen him at Instagram: @prasadbabugalla Your Quote: @prasadbabugalla

# Love and Goodness

Goodness is nothing but you,
It's stored inside you.
Goodness is always stronger than evil,
if you can't use proper way then it's a devil.

Love grows like a tree,
If your goodness makes everyone free
with victory of life which makes
things beautiful hugs and sweet kisses.

There is so much goodness inside you
and the dreams that are going to come true.
Goodness is love with burden
Which we can't simply abandon.

Even when golden days looks dark
if our goodness inside us without spark
Remember Goodness is inside you,
I promise you it's true!

# Love and Goodness

When your character alive,
Your goodness inside you is alive.
Goodness inside us acts
According to our kindness.

Goodness will always cherish it in my heart
and I thank you all for your support
which really means a lot
where there is no thought.

Love is not a goodness if
you went over the way of stiff.
Always give love and kindness,
Don't let their actions change your goodness.

Sharing each new day with loved ones
is the beautiful life with goodness.
Believe in your goodness,
which makes the people some usefulness?

# Love and Goodness

Your goodness is stronger than mountain,
which takes your love to fountain?
Your goodness is deeper than the sea
Which makes your kind heart to plea?

Never forget to spread love, light and kindness
in your beautiful life to be the goodness
and have a wonderful light
to brighten your heart.

Your goodness brings out
the goodness in inhabit.
Just set your heart on doing good
to get your life good.

Your goodness gains best friends
in the world of kindness
and you will be like a rainbow
of many colors and shadows.

# Love and Goodness

Your goodness will be visible
But your kind heart is invisible.
Your goodness inside you
is the energy of dew.

No need to prove your goodness
time will prove by your kindness.
Your goodness is the only investment
to make your life betterment.

Your seed of goodness
is found in the soil of appreciation.
It's a kind of beauty in the nature
And the wonder like mother.

# SHREYA POKHRIYAL

Shreya Pokhriyal is a college student who lives in dehradun and persuading her career as a writer is been 1 year. She loves exploring and learning new things.She is too small but started her career a way in 2019 by joining as a co-author in the book name 'Faded Memories'. It's her first anthology. She has been worked in 100+ anthologies. Her instagram handle is @An_anomalous_poet. The anthologies I had worked on are as follows Petrichor, Amor Patriae, next level attitude, Valentine's week book, logbook of 2020 and many more.

# Laugh of a New Born Baby...

A baby's first Laugh is so pure,
Which can make everything okay that's for sure.
Can even touch the most,
Brings back the happiness even it is lost.
Change the Hardened person turning them to softness,
By looking the baby's overloaded cuteness.
Oblivious to the world, they are
laughing even.
Yet touches our souls,
To fulfill even the uncompleted goals.
Bringing a tear to our eye!
Just looking which never let us utter the word bye.
No word of discouragement!
For a pure contentment.
A baby's laugh is so precious,
The finest wonder of the whole world.


# Always awake the goodness in you...

Always remember this..
No Matter how humble, nice or pure you gonna to be,
There will always be some..
People who will stab you directly in your heart
Despite you're showering them love and kindness..
They will hurt you by talking rubbish about you
They will laugh at you by making fun of u
Never I repeat.. Never I repeat..
Never let these people change good in u
Keep good thing alive in yourself

# Great Heights

The root way to your success
Where your aim are very high
The settlement is not easy you know why
It only depends upon your strive
Everyone is free to do it anything
None should be countered
What else can remain constant
The way of your step towards it
Even if you fall down
Get up and chase it again
The feeling of gratitude to admiring vanity
Down the line somewhere to the humanity
Don't be effortless ever,make a norm to dream
Mark my words as the actions which screams

# Happiness Mantra

One smile to start up a friendship.
One word to end up a fight.
One step to save a relation
One person to change your life.
One song to cheer you up.
One tear to change up your mood.
One wish to fulfill up a desire.
One way to set up a goal.
One breath to enjoy up a moment.
Just one but try once!!

# DEENDAYAL RAIKWAR

आपका नाम दीनदयाल रैकवार है, आप मत्स्य विभाग में जिला निरीक्षक पद पर कार्यरत हैं । आप जुवान के धनी हैं और सामाजिक न्याय के हित में काम करते हैं ।आप जिला झांसी उत्तर प्रदेश के रहने वाले हैं । आपने अभी तक का जीवन समाज की सेवा हेतु जिया है ।

# सोच

यदि मारना हो किसी को, तो मार दो एहसान से,
क्या मिलेगा मार कर, यदि मार दिया जान से ।
जान का मारा हुआ, दुश्मन बनेगा जान का,
सिर उठा नहीं सकता, मारा हुआ एहसान का ।।

दोस्त मैं आपको बता दूं कि हमारे सोसाइटी में माहौल इतना गंदा हो गया है कि लोग अपने पडोस की लडकी को भी गंदी नजर से देखते हैं, कहते हैं देखो बो जा रही है, कोई बोलता है भाभी है तेरी । मुझे एक बात समझ नहीं आती कि कोई ये क्यो नही कहता है कि बहिन है हमारी । ये बात तो तब समझ आयेगी जिस दिन उस जगह पर आपकी बहिन या बेटी होगी ।
यदि आज आप इज्जत करना नहीं सीखे, तो एक दिन आपकी कोई इज्जत नहीं करेगा । सभी को सम्मान देना सीखें, हर कोई चाहता है कि मेरी जिंदगी में अच्छे लोग आये, मुझे भी लोग अच्छा समझें, परन्तु दोस्त आप यदि अच्छी नजर से लोगों को देखते हैं तो पूरी दुनिया आपको अच्छी ही नजर आयेगी और यदि आप गंदी नजर से देखते हैं तो पूरी दुनिया आपको गलत ही लगेगी, इसीलिए आप अपनी सोच को बदलो, दुनिया अपने आप बदल जायेगी ।

# MEERA VYAS

She is Meera Vyas. She is 16 year old 11th grade Science student of Kameshwar Education Campus. She is a bright and sincere student. She lives in heritage city Ahmedabad. She likes travelling, camping, learning new launguages, listening songs and reading. She is very kind, socialized and open-minded person who is always eager to learn.

# कुछ ख़्याल ऐसे भी...

कभी कहीं रात को सोचना हुआ कि क्या है ज़िन्दगी?
लोगो को मेला या कहीं रात का अकेला?

जज़्बात के मलंग या प्यार मे कटी पतंग?

.
. हर रात में रोना होता है यहां,
हर बात पे समझौता होता है यहां।
"यहां हर मौसम मे गुनाह जायज़ है,
शायद इसीलिए उम्मीद पे दुनिया कायम है।"

क्या है ये ज़िन्दगी?

रातो का खयाल है ज़िन्दगी,
प्यार में बुरा हाल है ज़िन्दगी,
दोस्ती में तकरार है ज़िन्दगी,
आंसू मे भी मुस्कान है ज़िन्दगी,

बारिशों में धूप है ज़िन्दगी,
सुबह का नया रूप है ज़िन्दगी,

"वहीं होता है जो कभी ना सोचा होता है,
आखिर में होता वहीं है जो अच्छा होता है।"

आपबीती की कीमत क्या होगी?,
ख्वाईश की उम्मीद क्या होगी,।।
पहलू हरपर बढ़ाते रहे फासला मंज़िल का,
ज़िन्दगी के मुसाफिर कि खुशियां क्या होगी।

# SHAHEEN ANSARI

She is pursuing Masters in Microbiology. And the one who try to put her thoughts in words of her imaginary world with her unique viewpoint. She is a free soul of an utopia with a perspective of protopia. Her viewpoint to see the world have always been come up as the hog heaven were everything is just perfect and fulfilled. To connect with her through e-mail shahiin.ansarii@gmail.com and also Instagram - shahin_ansari_22

# Believe in Karma

May be somethings we learn are hypothesis,
It could be correct or wrong,
Vibes gives the impression of person,
It could be bad or good.

If we do good to others they do back too,
If they don't do good but God makes way to help us,
If we do bad to others they do back too,
If they don't do but God will makes way to hit us back.

Here what we can feel that karma hits its way back,
When people just don't believe in things,
Do good, good will happen to you,
Do bad, bad will lead to you anyhow.

That's how life works or can say God's way of doing,
What's right and what's not right for person,
So believe in God and have kindness within,
Do help and support everyone which would leads to better
for ownself.

# Where God lives ?

The Person with calmness and
Good morals and soul of truthful
In whom we can trust and believe
The one who never wish bad for someone.

The Person who has serenity within,
Who helps others without expecting in return,
In whom we can't find the wrong habits,
And can have faith on with all hearts.

May be that person could have done wrong,
But that makes them great student by learning right,
And unlearning what is not right that is
How good makes place in their soul.

God can reside in any person around,
We must also have to be one by
Doing good and spreading goodness
And by keeping faith on God's plan.

# Lord of Mercies

Sometimes I feel lost in the cage of emotions,
Where every side feels like I am trapped,
I feel alone in the path of life and then
I search for answers to my questions

That's when I ask God for solutions and also
Complain about not fulfilling my needs
But God never told that life would be easy,
But he did promised, he will never abandon

Somewhere within I find tranquillity because
I trust God that he will accompany me.
God's love sets me free and
His grace is sufficient for me

And I trust him wholeheartedly
I know God have perfect plan for me and
May I don't get that but it would be better.

# Goodness all around

Put me under the spell of calmness,
Let me sip the goodness from heaven,
Lighten up the sky with stars in night,
When receiving the illuminating shine of serenity.

Cover my body with the holy days and
Songs of praise that makes good vibes around,
Like the Happy girl playing with the doll
Who have the emotions which are natural and undeniable.

And let the fragrance of lily be spread all over,
So all can breathe the heavenly smell,
Of the kindness and love in the air,
Let the bitterness of thoughts left the world.

Bless me with the goodness of heart,
Bless me with the goodness of soul.

# PRATHAM MITTAL

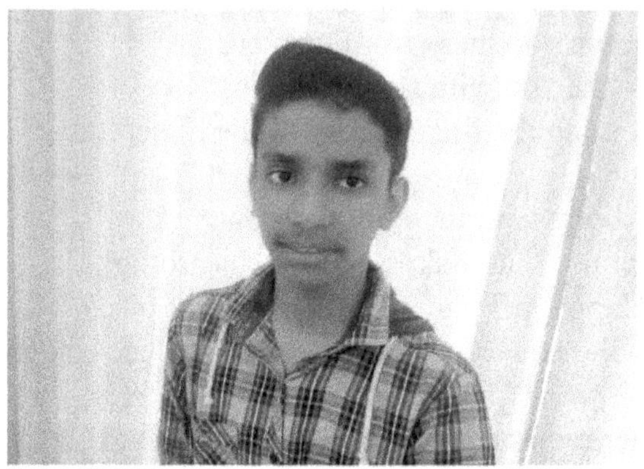

He is very Positive, kind, helpful, friendly and happy soul. His passion is painting and writing. He has won many competitions, He has Been Co-Authored of 55+ Anthology and has compiled 5+ Books in which one had recognized by **OMG Books of Record & Bravo International Book of World Records - Speaking My Truth**, Participated in International Writing Competitions.

# How Happy you're

I see the happiness on your smiley face
and the river flows through my eyes
I'm so helpless then hopeless!
and this heart weeps for missing my kins.

The world's heartless and that i lost my family
Yet I even have become stone hearted
How helpless i'm , oh indeed!
I'm unhappy, but acting like I'm happy
I'm the darkness and your eyes are filled with light!

You have a cheerful smile but I'm so sad,
Sometimes dream makes me scared,
Yeah, I'm so hopeless during this cruel world
How happy you're but I'm dying inside!

The morning involves your eyes, but I'm still in shock
But I'm still so helpless then thirsty of goodness.
Be with you the sunshine of peace forever
and I have devoted my Creator.

# HIMANSHI KAMBOJ

Hi,

It's Himanshi Kamboj. She is a 23 year old writer. She belongs to beautiful God's land uttarakhand, kashipur. She has completed her masters degree in physics. She is  martial art coach, social activist who works for the education of those children who lived in slum area. she has organised many free self defense camp for girls in government schools. She is the member of NGO 'Team Pankhuri'. Her hobbies are acting, dancing, martial art, painting, explore different cultures. She has written many quotes on different topics like Spirituality, Human Life, Nature, social issues, human empowerment, Mental illness etc.

# सच्ची खुशी

पंकज एक 25 साल का युवा लड़का था। आज उसके दिमाग मे अजीबोगरीब कसक चल रही थी। उसके द्वारा किया गया कार्य उसे याद आ रहा था। उसे ज़िंदगी में पहली बार आत्मिक सुख का अनुभव हुआ था। उसके मन में एक तरफ सुकून था, तो दूसरी तरफ एक अजीब सी कशमकस चल रही थी। पंकज को आज अपने बचपन के दिन याद आ रहे थे। वह एक मध्यमवर्गीय परिवार से था। उसके पिता किसान थे और माँ गृहिणी थी। खेती से ही उसके घर का गुजर-बसर होता था और दैनिक आवश्यकताओं की मुश्किल से पूर्ति होती थी। परंतु वो बचपन के दिन बहुत ही यादगार थे। उसके दोस्त राहुल और कृष्णा तो उसे आज भी याद हैं। उनके साथ स्कूल से आने के बाद गांव में अनेक खेल खेलना, वो स्वतंत्रता से भरी मौज-मस्ती, गांव के वो पुराने दिन उसे याद आ रहे थे। पंकज एक होनहार बच्चा था। अपने पिता को कठिन परिश्रम करते हुए देखकर उसने ठान ली थी कि वह एक दिन अपनी किस्मत बदलकर रहेगा।

उसने 12वीं में अच्छे अंक प्राप्त किए और एक इंजी. कॉलेज से अपनी पढ़ाई पूरी की। जल्दी ही उसकी नौकरी एक अच्छी कम्पनी में लग गई, जहाँ से उसे अच्छा वेतन मिलता था। परंतु कुछ समय पश्चात वह इस नौकरी से ऊबने लगा। प्रतिदिन उसे यह बात परेशान करती थी कि भले ही वह एक अच्छी कम्पनी में नौकरी करता है, जहाँ से वेतन भी लाखों में मिलता है, परंतु वह यह सोचकर चिंतित रहता था कि जिंदगी की भागदौड़ में उसे भी भागना है। इस भागदौड़ भरी ज़िन्दगी का उस पर बुरा असर पड़ा, कुछ बुरी आदतों ने उसे जकड़ लिया। कभी-कभी हम इस भागदौड़ भरी ज़िन्दगी में अपने दिल की खुशी को कब भुला देते हैं, पता ही नहीं चलता। एक दिन पंकज अपनी नौकरी के लिए बस में जा रहा था, तभी उसे एक बच्चे ने आवाज दी।
भैया, "एक कप चाय पियोगे क्या? "

पंकज ने पूछा - कितने रुपये का एक कप चाय है?

10 रुपये का, लड़के ने उत्तर दिया।

पंकज ने कहा - लाओ, एक कप चाय दे दो।

उसके बाद पंकज ने उस लड़के से पूछा - बेटा, तुम पढ़ने के लिए स्कूल नहीं जाते क्या?

लड़का बोला - भैया, मैं गरीब हूँ। पेट भरने के लिए पास के ही एक ढाबे पर काम करता हूँ, उससे जो भी कमाई होती है, मेरे खाने का इंतज़ाम हो जाता है। बच्चे ने मायूसी आवाज़ में कहा।

पंकज बोला - क्या तुम मुझसे पढ़ोगे?

मैं कल तुम्हें पढ़ाने आऊंगा।

जब उसने यह बात उस बच्चे से बोली तो बच्चे के चेहरे पर एक चमक भरी मुस्कान आ गई। अगले ही दिन अपनी नौकरी जाने के एक घंटे पहले वह उस बच्चे को पढ़ाने पहुँच गया। धीरे-धीरे उसने आस-पास के बच्चों के साथ समय बिताना शुरू कर दिया और साथ ही मुफ्त में पढ़ाना भी। अब पंकज को आत्मिक शान्ति व सुख का अनुभव होने लगा। उसे आत्मसंतुष्टि होती कि वह दूसरों के जीवन में बदलाव ला रहा है। इससे पंकज की सभी बुरी आदतें दूर हो गईं। उसने संकल्प किया कि वह अब गरीब और अनाथ बच्चों की शिक्षा के लिए कार्य करेगा। अंततः उसने नौकरी छोड़ दी और एक अनाथालय खोला और बच्चों की शिक्षा के लिए कार्य करना आरंभ कर दिया।

जिंदगी में भलाई का कार्य ही आपको आत्मिक सुख और शांति देता है। किसी के जीवन में बदलाव लाइए और भलाई के कार्य कीजिये। ये अनंत ब्रह्माण्ड आपको सच्ची खुशी और शांति देगा। दुनिया में मानवता ही सबसे बड़ा धर्म है।

# JASMINE PANDA

Miss Jasmine Panda is presently pursuing M.Sc. Chemistry from Berhampur University, Bhanjabihar, Odisha, India. She is a Gold Medalist and University Topper in her B.Sc. She was also the M.Sc. Entrance Topper in BU. She is also continuing an internship CSIR-SRTP in IICT Hyderabad. She holds the post of Senate Member of the University for the session 2019-20 in Academic Pursuits. She is a Governor Awardee for Youth Red Cross. She has received All-Rounder Award in her 12th standard for excellence in extracurricular activities along with studies. She is a Topper throughout her career. She has been Literary and Cultural Champion in her college days. She has also cracked a campus in Vedanta. She has hosted in numerous events including International events and has been appreciated as an anchor. She has completed Masters in Fine Arts (MFA) from Aurobindo Kala Bhawan under Bangeeya Sangeet Parishad. Besides, she has also done a computer course PGDCA. Apart from being a versatile orator and debator, she has been a part of 230+ anthologies till now and loves to pen down her feelings! She is an amiable person interested in both Science and Literature, having a wide variety of interests like painting, sketching, acting, anchoring, debating, rangoli making, taking part in extempore, elocution and many more...Publishing her own book someday is something which she aspires.

# सामाजिक बनना अभी बाकी है....

समाज में रहकर हम,
शायद सामाजिक बनना बाकी है!
सामाजिक बनना अभी बाकी है....

अंधविश्वासों पर आंखें बंद करके भरोसा,
भक्तों से पैसे लेना अब हो गया है पेशा।
करते हैं सामाजिक रीति-नीति का पालन,
सही गलत का न करके हम अवलोकन।

पुण्य तिथियों पर साफ़-सफ़ाई का कार्यक्रम,
ये न करो, वो न करो, हो जाता है भ्रम।
"लोग क्या कहेंगे?" सबको है इसका डर,
यही सोच-सोच कर फोड़ते हैं अपना सर।

अपनी सामाजिक स्तिथि बनाए रखने के लिए,
कामचोर बनकर मंदिर में जलाते हैं दिए।
अपनाते हैं कुछ, सोचते विविध उपाय,
थोड़ा सा कुछ हुआ विचार करते समुदाय।

सामाजिक अव्यव्स्था से घेरे हुए हैं हम,
लेकिन दूसरों को मज़ा चखाकर लेते हैं दम।
हुई कुछ अनहोनी, करते समाज पर दोसारोप,
भूल जाते हैं हमसे ही तो बना है सामाजिक स्वरूप।

इसलिए तो समाज में रहकर हम
शायद सामाजिक बनना बाकी है!
सामाजिक बनना अभी बाकी है.....

# Unconditional Love

The love and affection of my parents,
The struggle they do for me,
The hardwork they do day and night,
The patience they have in every situation,
The motivation they give me in every situation,
The perfect kind of role models for me,
The ones who go to any extent for me,
The ones who fulfill every dream of mine,
The ones who can devote their life for me,
The ones who think of nothing else than me!
For them, I am their world,
For me, they are my world!
The love and affection of my parents,
Is seriously unconditional....

The love and affection of my grandparents,
The extreme care they have for me,
The serious they are for my health,
The extent to which they can be strict with my parents for me,
The dreams they see for me,
The madness after seeing their grandchildren so long,
The blessings that they shower everytime,
The happiness they feel cooking for us,
The stories and moral lessons they share,
The values they try to inculcate,
The prosperity that they want to see,
The successful lives they have imagined for us,
The love and affection of my grandparents,
Is seriously unconditional...

The love and affection of my cousins,
The childish fights we do for chocolates, for toys...

The memories that grew up with our age,
The little things for which we cry,
The craziness that we are fond of,
The enjoyment that we find in every serious issue!
The care we show for each other,
The vacation plannings we do together,
The amazing childhood days we did share,
Growing up to be professional, still fighting for little things,
The behaviour that we show as kids! Maturity at its extreme...
The love and respect we have for each other,
The love and affection of my cousins,
Is seriously unconditional...
Is seriously unconditional...

# SIMON CHIATANTE

"Simon Chiatante was born in the South of Italy. After his Master's degree in Translation Studies in Scotland he changed his life completely, moving to China and working as a teacher. He is the author of 'Floating Petals', a collection of poems and editor of 'Watch Movies Learn Languages', a language learning manual by Ashton Jones."

# (1)

The room is dim and hushed
after the town is half
done for today
at noon the workers rest
the family members nap
or think, or write
at the constant tickle of the clock
ever present in their life
even at night, when it's
determined to make it even
with the day
in a continuous flow
and if you think deeper
it's never stopped
only when you had to change
it's batteries or fix it
but then it just keeps pulsing
as it was only muted
and on and on
until the end of time
but what it's good of all this
is what is left on the paper
just there..

**(2)**

Asleep and cold
the forest and the reeds,
the soot black shadow underneath,
a moonless night
wrapped in the dark

And yet it seems
that something breathes
unseen, above, the billowed
clouds, the frozen sky,
the glowing weeds,
the grass that's waving light;

Far in the East,
a glimmer grows
in flashing rays, the sun
embracing all that's dark,
expanding to the hills and plains.
Wakes everything again.

**(3)**

How many times
you've opened that old drawer
in your house, full
of scratch-paper and pages,
old broken objects put there
maybe to be forgotten,
that kind of limbo
where they can't be totally
thrown away
but neither be seen.

And how many times
you've seen and read those, then
you've been caught by the randomly
blended series of odours lost
and lost you have yourself
with them
and you've thought of
how good it was
how foolish to neglect
how careless to forget.

**(4)**

How long it's been
since you've opened it?
How long will it be
until you open it again?
Good memories
are presents now,
so now how much better
are you gonna be?

# MS DAKSHA R. UDHANI

Miss Daksha Rajeshkumar udhani daughter of Mr Rajeshkumar udhani and Mrs Simran udhani, a phd (doctorate ) student and even a passionate writer, her writing journey started when she was a school going child, she is such a soul who express every feeling by penning down her emotions on the paper, it is said that sometimes the person is unable to speak and express his or her feelings but it can be expressed in a writing format, currently she is working on 30+

Anthologies and even has complied 4 books on her own, in a very short span she has crossed many ladders and reached a step ahead to the success, soon the books are going to launch hence we believe that every poetry written by her touches the readers mind and soul hope these ones also touch the readers mind and soul..

Insta I'd - @chefoholic_

# **Goodness in nature**

I find goodness in the lap of nature,
Making the soul feathery and filmsy,
Blossoms of numerous shades,
Red, white & pink Roses appearing adorable,
 gorgeous glance of daffodil,
 melodious songs of fowls,
Fauna grazing merrily in the meadow,
Flora striking at the Shore,
 that marvelous nightfall,
When water begins to gleam,
 and the Luna approaches.

# Goodness

As the beauty of life is in the stages of life to see to admire the would to experience it.

Stages of life reflects the stairs of the terrace with a step anthor stage with new challenge and opportunity at every step are waiting by the door opening.

There are many stages of life like birth childhood teenage , youth and old-age but the best and unique is the teenage.

Teens period is that part of one's life when he has knowledge of everything but same time he gets affected frequently others like fashions chilling with friends and much more things.

Their stage is very crucial stage of to festive as their present will affect their life in future.

So there is a very need in shaping their future so maintain a positive environment around…

# PRESENCE OF GOODNESS

Talking about goodness
Meant me everything
The credit, we are alive
Hoping to wake up again
For a better tomorrow

Goodness remains hidden
In everything
Around ourself
Whether it be nature or human being

Looking at the natural beauties
Love birds enchanting
"Look at those cuties,
Sweet and high pitched chirping"

Gazing at the clear sky
A marvellous and heavenly combo
Do you want to know why?
The little twinkling  stars and the white jumbo

Goodness thrives everywhere
I see it embroidered
On each "Hard-ware" As because of them, I wondered..

# Art of goodness

G - go and workship the god ask him for the blessings,
O - open the new day with the beautiful smiles,
O - optain the positive energy from your parents,
D - do what your soul says is right
N - negatives will come across your path but,
E - eventually make the decision which helps you to motivate and gives you the strength
S - shine more bright like a sun,
S - slowly gradually you will cross all the ladders and reach the success goals..

And thus this stage will make uh a good and a successful person in your life.. stay strong and keep kindness and goodness all among yourself..!!

Flairs and Glairs, a platform by a student for the students. We are esteemed youth struggling to carve out our path for our future and we follow a basic mindset Since everyone is not born with all-round skills. Joining hands with people who are born to execute it with perfection is the best way to evolve. Self-Evolution is the need of the hour but, evolving as a community is what we strive for. The initiative as kickstarted by, Founder- Mr. Shubham Shah with the motive to utilize the skillset and talent of writing has now a team of 10+ people who are actively participating into newer forms of learning and discovering talents among youngsters. We Provide platform and services like Publishing opportunities, Open mics, Workshops, Hands-on training. Operating with Brand Name of Flairs and Glairs (Publication House), we offer the chance of elevating a passionate writer to an esteemed author With Brand name Teekhe Zasbaaat. We bring to you an opportunity to get accustomed with the Public Speaking and Presenting of Thoughts along with regular challenges to brush up your inking spirit. The newest initiative to extend our services we introduced in a new writing Platform- The Glittering Fables and Ink Over Tears.

*We Choose to Fly Like A Falcon than to be*

*a Leg Pulling Crab.*

To Know More:  Infoline – 7781900870
Mail Us At-
flairsandglairs@gmail.com / info@flairsandglairs.in
Or Visit is at
www.flairsandglairs.com / www.flairsandglairs.in
Social Handles- @flairsandglairs @teekhezasbaaat